No Choice and Other Stories

Femdom Mind Control

Flash Fiction – Vol. 33

S.B.

Table of Contents

Nowhere to go except trance.

Thank you to all patrons of Spell... B-O-U-N-D.

Decisive Moment

Greg stopped in front of the private elevator that led to his boss's suite. Barbara Harris had always been a woman of many charms even before he joined her law firm, but now she had taken it one step further. He had no one to blame but himself though he couldn't do it and keep a straight face. Everything was too exciting, the perfect opportunity to finally let go of his fears and prejudices. There was still time to go back and try to forget the triggers within, yet that would be such a waste. Using the key she had left in the top drawer of his desk the day before, he got in and began his ascension into mesmerizing greatness.

The music inside wasn't the same low-key cookie-cutter stuff he was used to, but something special. It had the same harmonies as the videos he had been engrossed with for the last three weeks, an unexpected melody that could simultaneously dull his brain and make his arousal go haywire. It comprised only six notes, but they played off each other so perfectly that his thoughts melted away with each repetition.

When the elevator finally stopped and the doors opened to let him out, the lawyer who was on the wrong side of forty, took a deep breath and nearly lost it when Barbara welcomed him in a skintight latex catsuit that had no business looking so good on her as it did. Despite being a year older than him, in that stunning combo that made every curve in her body explode in pure delight, she could almost pass as his daughter.

"You came..." she purred. "I was hoping you would, but there was always a small chance for a surprising surge of resistance. I'm happy to know you're as weak-minded as I thought. Come closer."

Greg took a couple of steps forward, every muscle in his body tingling. Everything felt like an absurdly erotic dream come to life, only this was one he didn't want to wake up from. As soon as he stopped moving, she continued,

"So... what part of my videos did you enjoy the most? My sexy parades in full body tight costumes like the one I'm wearing right now? My sultry looks at the camera as I played with my exposed pussy? No, I think it was the first time I used the words 'hypnosis', 'domination', and 'control' and you took notice of what I was really trying to pull off and still kept on watching, willingly handing over your mind and body to my spellbinding trance. Warm or not?"

Scorching. Not even a dozen volcanoes erupting at the same time could compare to that magnetic pull. Thinking of hypnosis had always been his demise, and now his fantasies had come full circle. His cock shot upwards like a ship's mast ready to face the most violent storm of all.

"Hmmm... lovely. And I bet that at that decisive moment you were baffled how I guessed your innermost desires, the ones you told no one out of fear and shame," Barbara purred again as she licked his right ear. "Well, let me satisfy your curiosity, sweetie. You forgot to clean your browsing history the last time you were adrift in your fantasies at work, and so you ended up telling me everything I needed to know to make you mine. It's a good thing we both wanted the same as it sure made things a lot easier."

Greg nodded and turned his head to follow her, hoping for a stray kiss that never came. Perhaps in time, if he proved himself worthy...

"And now, my dear pet, you never have to dream about losing your will to a superior woman again because you've already done so. You can thank me as many times as you want by dropping to your knees and not standing up unless I command it."

He sank hard, head buried between her latex crotch. Perfection was no longer a mirage, but the pure reality dripping in his soul. Happily, he drifted deeper and deeper under her hypnotic power.

Don't Open This File

Gail stood inside a perfect replica of her college dorm, trying hard not to look at the brightly lit laptop screen that demanded her attention. It had only been one hour since the twenty-year-old violet-haired wannabe musician had agreed to take part in the experiment, and she was already regretting it. She glanced nervously across the room, her eyes sometimes catching a reflection of the camera lenses tracking her every movement. Dr. Rawlins was sure to be enjoying her torment.

The experiment comprised a simple test of curiosity and impulse control. For the next twenty-four hours, she had to stay indoors. She could do whatever she wanted in this familiar environment, except one thing.

"See this video file on your computer?" the doctor had said. "You are not to open it under any circumstances."

"What's in it?"

"The point is for you not to know. Refrain from succumbing to the temptation of finding out and we'll cover your tuition for the rest of the year."

"Sounds easy enough. I'll just turn off the computer, unplug it, and the money is as good as mine," Gail responded.

"Cute, but I'm afraid you can't do that. The laptop will be on the whole time, and the file ready to be opened with a single click. Of course, that won't be a problem to you, right?"

"Right."

It was amazing how wrong she was. The moment the experiment began, the file was all she could think of, like a forbidden fruit in technological form. There it was, in the dead center of a pulsating screen, as if calling her name. "Don't open me," it whispered. "Even though you really want to."

Yes, she did. It should have been easy to go with the flow and entertain herself with the vast array of objects at her disposal. She had a pile of sexy books, a TV, a state-of-the-art gaming console, and yet all she wanted to know was the reason behind such secrecy. Was there really something important in the video or was it just a trap?

She waited, and waited, and waited. After the three-hour mark, she was already biting her nails to keep herself together. There was no way she would last another twenty-one, and it's not like it was that much money to begin with, so...

"Fuck it! I want to know," she said as she reached for the laptop mouse and hit the video file. At first, there was only a blank screen punctuated by some ominous music in the background. Then, the image faded into a frontal view of Dr. Emma Rawlins and her tantalizing cleavage reprimanding her.

"You had to do it, didn't you?" she said. "Even after all the warnings, you had to open it. You were told not to, but you couldn't let go. While a bit of curiosity can be a good thing, if it stops you from making good decisions then it must be put under control. This has always been the primary point of this experiment. You've allowed yourself to temporarily lose control of your emotions and now, we'll be fixing that. Your brain will be rebooted to focus only on the right things, like all the students that came before you and all the ones still left to come. When we're done, everyone on campus will have a perfectly balanced mind, unhindered by any distractions. Listen to my voice, Gail, and learn..."

The video turned into a spectacle of intersecting spirals where all colors of the rainbow conspired to make her eyes feel tired and drowsy and in the center of the chromatic confusion, laid the clarity of Dr. Rawlins' ideas, telling her how to act and feel.

Good students don't think.

Good students don't get distracted.

Good students obey their teachers and learn their lessons well.

Good students never let their curiosity control their actions.

Good students don't question what they're taught.

Good students are always ready to do what Dr. Rawlins wants.

"Will you be a good student for me, Gail?"

Yes. She had failed a simple task once, but not this time. She would never fail again. All the files in her mind were being put in locked boxes, and only the doctor held the key. As long as she remained in charge, they would never be open again.

Hostile Takeover

Francis got out of his car under a heavy blanket of rain and entered the main building of Blackwood Industries. Pamela Blackwood, the woman he was going to meet, was one of the most successful and powerful entrepreneurs in the States in the last decade. He had heard countless tales about her aggressive business tactics but was far from imagining just how devious she could be.

It was exactly one minute past 7 pm when he entered her office, his suit in disarray and brown hair dripping on the carpet. Not the most promising of starts for such an important meeting, but what could he do? He was shocked when he saw her all dressed in black and holding a whip in both hands, and even more when she offered him a cold stare as if she were on a higher plane of existence.

"Miss Blackwood, thank you for seeing me," he mumbled. "As discussed over the phone, I have here with me my consortium's proposal for the acquisition of your shoe factory in New England," he laid down his briefcase on her desk and opened it. "If you would be so kind to take a look…"

"Quiet!" she replied, eyes focused on something he couldn't quite tell what it was. If she was trying to intimidate him, there was no doubt she was being successful.

"Something the matter?" he asked, trying to ignore her eccentricities. Patricia was only thirty-one years old, but had the maturity and business savvy of someone twice her age. She was also used to getting whatever she wanted and right now she demanded silence.

"Before we move on to the boring stuff, we have more important things to discuss."

"We do?"

"Yes," she looked down at him again like an angry teacher about to reprimand a student and waved the whip back and forth.

It was a slow movement at first, perfectly restrained by her dexterous hands. He followed it intently wondering what she was trying to pull off. Suddenly, she began waving it faster, darting from left to right and right to left, a living blur manifesting before his confused gaze.

"Is there a point to this, Miss Blackwood?"

"Just stare for now. Do it right and you'll soon find out."

He did as commanded lest she became upset. It wasn't the first time he did something strange to secure a business deal, and it wouldn't be the last either. He focused on every sweeping gesture, his pupils in sync with every twist and turn. As he kept staring, his vision tunneled, shadows forming in the corners of his eyes. An overpowering need to look deeper and deeper grew within him like a drug until there was only her face and her whip... her face and her whip... her face and...

"Sleep," she touched his forehead with the tip of her BDSM toy, sending his already befuddled brain down an ever-growing pit of helplessness.

Francis nodded, though he did so involuntarily. His body was now responding to her stimuli alone, his simple trance state becoming stronger and more irresistible with every breath he took.

"Perfect..." she purred. "This is what I was talking about. Do you know why my empire grew so much in the last couple of years? It's because I only do business with easily suggestible men, and you've just shown me what material you're made of. You should know I've decided not to sell the factory after all, but I'll keep you as my hypno-slave to help me plan a hostile takeover of your consortium. Do you agree?"

"Yes," he meekly replied, dropping to his knees. If you were in his shoes, I'm sure you would have done the same.

I'm Not a Slave

Brandon walked around back and forth in his bedroom, a single thought on his mind. It was a simple thing, something that would never cross other people's thoughts (at least not anyone he knew!), but he had to repeat it time and time again to not risk going insane. That thought was:

"I'm not a slave."

He wasn't. Never! No matter what Caroline told him, regardless of any scheme - direct or indirect - to convince him of his inferiority towards her, he would always stand his ground. He had ideas of his own and free will to execute them. He was not a slave!

Caroline... how could he have been so wrong about her? For six months, he tried so hard to be a part of her circles, to know what she liked and disliked, and the best way to win her over. There was something about the early thirties redhead with the body of a water nymph that made him want to jump through every hoop imaginable to please her. And then, right after getting hooked, she had ruined it all by trying to emasculate him.

"Don't you think I'm a Goddess?" she had told him one night after a very expensive dinner - the third in two weeks! - he had paid for, of course. "Goddesses deserve to be pampered and, better yet, served. You'll serve me well, won't you, my little slave?"

At first, he had looked upon her remark as nothing but a joke even though no one laughed. It was only after she started hammering the idea with brainwashing cues and menial assignments he had to fulfill to remain in her good graces that he realized how the game was being played. She made the rules and changed them as she pleased. If he didn't adjust, he was out.

"Slaves never complain," she concluded. "Just obey."

"But I'm not a slave!" he muttered as he continued to wear down the bedroom's carpet. "Fuck! I'm not a slave!"

"Oh, you silly boy... that's all you've ever been and all you can hope to be in her world," the other voice that lived inside him replied. It was a recent construct, planted by her somehow. He suspected hypnosis but wasn't sure. He was never certain of anything when he saw her perfect crimson lips.

"Shut up! You're not real!" Brandon spat.

"The only thing that isn't real is the fact that you're doubting her. Instead of rejoicing for having found your destiny, you're stuck in your house on a weekend, badmouthing your owner! Does that sound natural to you? Stop resisting her. That's an order!"

"I said, shut up!" he suddenly stopped and banged his head against the wall. Blood dripped from his forehead and onto his striped, blue shirt. "Go away already! I'm not a slave. I'm not a slave!"

"The longer you fight the longer I'll be around. Goddess Caroline is all you need. Relinquish your foolish thoughts of independence before it's too late."

"NO!" he screamed so loud that he was sure to have woken up the neighbors.

"We'll see who's right in the end," the mellifluous persona grinned inside his brain. "I'm too powerful already. I'm not going anywhere."

Brandon leaned his back against the wall and dropped to the floor, sobbing. It was going to be another restless night torn between two competing truths. He wasn't a slave, but when she looked at him and batted her long eyelashes, every inch of his body longed to kneel at her feet and be stomped by dangerous heels until he bled. Fuck. Fuck! FUCK!

"Center yourself," he mumbled. "Come on, you can do it again. I know you can."

Not this time. The Saturday night dragged on as he withered into absolute nothingness. The other self would soon return to steal his life and soul. He was a slave. He would obey her forever.

In My Humble Opinion

Mark loved Camilla. From the day they had first met, courtesy of a mutual friend, she had always been everything he expected from a woman, a true dream given form. The South American beauty was sweet and caring, had the same sense of humor as him, and never complained about his manly hobbies even if she hated them with a passion. She respected his boundaries and he respected hers, thus creating a solid foundation for a relationship that could potentially last forever.

As time went by, the connection that bound them grew stronger, yet a small detail began haunting his state of mind. As much as he adored her, there was a sentence she said on a regular basis that ticked him off and he had no idea why. The sentence was,

"In my humble opinion..."

Hearing it once? No problem. Hearing it twice or three times in the same day? A bit strange, but okay. Hearing it all the time they were having a conversation? Annoying as fuck, especially given what always seemed to happen afterward. He hated to admit it, but he had had enough.

"We need to talk," he said one day as they were returning home from a night at the theater.

"Do we really?"

"Yes. I've been postponing it for a while, but I have to get this out of my chest before it drives me insane. Will you please listen?"

"Of course, sweetie," Camila smiled. "What's on your mind?"

"It's something you say. You use this expression a lot and it's starting to grate on my nerves. I was wondering if you could tone it down a bit going forward."

"What expression is that?"

"In my humble opinion..."

"You don't like it when I say that?"

"I don't like to hear you say it all the time."

"But I don't do that."

"Yes, you do. Just today, you've said it when we were deciding what movie to watch, what type of popcorn I should buy, whether we should call a cab or an Uber... it's annoying."

"Are you saying you don't like it when I voice my opinions?"

"No, that's not at all. You just don't have to say the same thing over and over again. It's almost like..."

"Like what?"

"Like you're programming my mind or something. This is weird as fuck, I know, but I couldn't help but notice that every time you say that I always end up agreeing with you."

"And why is that a bad thing? You love agreeing with me."

"It's... confusing. I don't ask for much from you, but I'm asking you this: for the sake of my sanity, keep those words to a minimum, okay?"

"I see what's going on. Do you want to hear what I think?"

"Sure."

"In my humble opinion, you're a bit tired and cranky today."

"Fuck! You've just said it again."

"In my humble opinion, getting all riled up with me over something I say isn't going to take you anywhere."

"Hmmm... could you please...?"

"In my humble opinion, it would be best if you stopped talking right now and simply listen to my words. You will do that, won't you?"

Mark nodded, mouth slightly ajar. His thought patterns had slowed down to a crawl as his girlfriend continued arranging his mind.

"In my humble opinion, questioning me is wrong. I don't think you should do that ever again. You value my opinions and are always happy to let me do the thinking for you. There's no point in changing what works, so why bother? You agree, correct?"

His head bobbed slightly forward like a spring doll.

"Good. In my humble opinion, these last five minutes never happened. I've forgotten about them. When I snap my fingers, so will you, and then we can go back to the way everything was before. This is what I want, so...

snap

Mark loved Camilla. She was the most beautiful woman ever. He was so lucky to have her in control of his life!

"Was I saying something?" he muttered, lost in her lovely aquamarine eyes.

"I don't think so. Was there something you wanted to say?"

"No."

"Good. I do though. Want to listen?"

"Of course."

"In my humble opinion, you should worship my pussy all night long the moment we arrive home."

Her opinions were the best.

No Choice

Sandra Harris sat in a private interrogation room at the USP Atwater, California, recorder laid on the cold metal table. Despite trying to keep a cool exterior, the near-thirties raven-haired journalist was quite excited. It was the first time she was interviewing a murderer, let alone such a noteworthy one. Former Detective Randall Dawson had been the man in charge of the homicide investigation of oil tycoon Eli Glenn before confessing the deed himself in a surprise twist that had taken the whole media outlets by storm. During his trial, Dawson offered a detailed account of everything that transpired and the reasons behind the crime, leaving the jury with no other choice than to sentence him to a minimum of twenty-five years.

Even after being locked away for half a decade, Dawson remained a surprisingly athletic man with a face straight out of a fashion magazine. In his days at the force, he had been voted twice as the most eligible bachelor, and even after stabbing a man forty-seven times to death, some still saw him as quite the catch. Sandra fit in that lot though she would never say it out loud.

He sat before her, hands and feet tightly chained, making it impossible for him to move. Usually, interviews required at least one guard in the room, but Sandra's editor had pulled some strings in the background. The two were alone inside, with the guards waiting by the door. Half an hour was the allotted time, so she had to make it count.

"Good morning, Mr. Dawson. My name is Sandra and on behalf of *CityBuzz*, I would like to thank you for agreeing to this interview."

"No need for that," he grumbled. "It's not like I had a choice."

"There's always a choice."

"Not in my case. Shall we get started? I would like to return to my cell as quickly as possible."

"Certainly. Tomorrow marks the sixth anniversary of the death of Eli Glenn, and even though you've answered this before, the public would like to know if the passage of time affected your reasoning or not, so... why did you do it?"

"I didn't," he replied somberly.

"Excuse me?"

"I didn't commit the crime I'm here for. I'm not a murderer and I'll never be one."

"Interesting... that's not what you've been saying all along and what the evidence determined. Why are you changing your story after all this time?"

"Because my perspective on this matter has never been clearer. It's surprising how isolation is such a powerful tool to clear one's mind of nefarious influences."

"Not sure I understand what you mean. Care to elaborate? If you didn't commit the crime, then who did?"

"Laura Glenn, of course."

"The widow?"

"Yes. I'm sure you did your research before coming here, so you know she was once a prime suspect before the murder weapon was found in my place. She killed him and manipulated me to take the blame, and I fell for it. At the time, I had no choice but to."

"I'm confused. Manipulated you how?"

"Hypnosis, brainwashing, mind-warping techniques galore... she used it all on me when I started investigating the case. That's how I ended up in her bed, too."

"What? You're now admitting you had an affair with the widow as well?"

"We had something going on for sure, but I wouldn't call it an affair. Sex was her way of keeping me close so she could get inside my head and play me to take the blame. It worked as intended because I'm stuck in here now and she's out there married to some other rich guy who'll probably end up dead sooner or later too."

Sandra tapped the edge of the table and said, "That's quite the story, Mr. Dawson."

"Not just a story, but the truth. "

"If so, then why are you only bringing that up today? Why not when you were first questioned, trialed, and then incarcerated?"

He let out a loud exhale. "Because I was still heavily brainwashed back then and didn't remember the details. In my mind, I was convinced I was guilty and deserved to be punished for my actions. Now, I can see all the ruses clearly and I know what went wrong. I don't expect you to believe me, but I wanted to get this off my chest and now I did, so thanks."

Sandra turned off the recorder and smirked, "Oh, but I do believe you."

"You do?"

"Yes, and so the next part of this interview is off-the-record," she gently lowered her voice. "Mistress Laura sends her regards."

"Huh?" his eyes widened. "You're in cahoots with that whore?"

"I serve her like you once did," Sandra crossed her legs under the table. "Mistress has suspected for a while that your mind was back to normal and when she heard of this opportunity, my assignment became clear. I was going to push you as hard as I could to get you to reveal your true feelings, but you did that on your own and made everything easier. Too bad no one will believe you now, right?"

"Why, you filthy little bitch! Tell that skank our story isn't over yet. One day, I'll get even!"

"Kind of hard to in your situation but I'll pass along your message just for laughs... Well done, Mr. Dawson. You truly were quite the puppet."

Sandra grabbed the recorder and walked away from the table under his angry, watchful gaze. She laughed on the inside as he struggled against the chains hoping for a little payback that would never come. Mistress Laura would be proud of her, and there was nothing better than that.

Old Trigger

Tracy and Carmen sat together in the latter's favorite bar, one Vodka shot away from crossing their alcoholic intake for the night when the young Nubian Goddess looked past her friend's black curly locks and said,

"Hey, girlfriend... I spy with my little eye a cute little thing that hasn't stopped looking at you since he arrived. I wonder if you know him?"

"Oh?" Carmen stole a glance across the bar and giggled. "Oh, it's him! Yeah, I know him. His name is Rob, or Bob, or... whatever. I remember we hooked up a couple of times and that he had this strange sexual fantasy."

"Define strange." Tracy pursed her cherry-painted lips.

"He kept talking about how he wanted to be hypnotized into becoming a slave and submit to whatever I desired. He was willing to do anything to be put under, go figure!"

"That's certainly different, but I bet it could be a lot of fun too, so what did you do?"

"Well, one day I decided to play along, so I bought a pair of contact lenses and one of those prismatic pendulums and had him meet me in my place. When he arrived, I dimmed the lights and put on the best performance of my life, telling him he was now under my power and had to do whatever I commanded. The weirdest thing is that it actually worked! From that day forward, whenever I wanted something from him, all I had to do was say these special trigger words and... *voilà*, instant slave!"

"You're joking!"

"No, it really happened, but it wasn't as fun as you think. While I had some great moments with him between my legs, one day I got tired of it all and it was all over. I never saw him again until today."

"Did you at least undo the trigger?"

"No. Why bother? I figured he would forget it, eventually."

"What if he didn't?"

"What are you saying?"

"What if you were to call him over, say the words, and see how he reacts?"

"Why would I do that?"

"Because he's darn cute, and I would love to fuck his mind over the weekend. Can we?" Tracy batted her long eyelashes. "Please?"

"Are you serious?"

"Honey, do you realize just how wet you made my pussy after that story of yours? Damn right, I'm serious! Do him once more and if it's as hot as I'm sure it will be, I'll even let you do me too."

Carmen smirked. Well, that was something new! She had never told her about such things before because she was convinced she wouldn't be into them, but that level of enthusiasm spoke volumes. Sitting with her legs crossed, she imagined herself dusting off the old lenses and slowly draining her will to resist while Rob/Bob/Whatever licked their feet clean... Hmmm, yes, that could work...

"Are you game or not?" Tracy slid her left hand under the table and up her leather skirt.

"Let's do it," Carmen nodded as she addressed the enraptured man. "Oh my God, it's you! It's been so long! Care to join us for a drink?"

Rob/Bob/Whatever gulped and headed for their table, believing that Lady Fortune was finally smiling at him once more.

"*Magic Unicorn*," Carmen cooed, and his mind went blank. He would remember nothing of the next two days except occasional glimpses of the two women making out atop his giant metal cage.

One Hell of a Business

Dave was not in a good mood. Then again, that was no surprise. His patience had been running on fumes ever since the day Ava, his long-term girlfriend had told him it "was probably for the best if they started seeing other people". The revelation had caught him completely off-guard, turning dreams of old into nightmares he couldn't get rid of. Anyone that came to talk to him after that incident had to be prepared to deal with his mood swings or else...

When he opened the front door of his apartment that Friday morning and saw the elegant brunette dressed in a three-piece navy-blue suit and wearing the darkest sunglasses he had ever seen, the first words that came out of his half-sleepy mouth were, "Whatever it is you're selling, I'm not interested. Go away!"

"Oh, I'm not a saleswoman, Mr. Sanders. Your bank sent me to discuss what's going on with your mortgage," she smiled. "May I come in?"

"No, you may not. I received your letter and will deal with the situation next week, so if you'll excuse me..."

"I do not," she pushed her left foot forward, preventing him from closing the door. "It's been 'next week' for you for almost three months now and that's frankly unacceptable. We're having this conversation today, Mr. Sanders, whether you want it or not."

"Oh, really?" he cracked a fist. "That sounded like a threat, and I hate being threatened. Please leave before I get mad."

"I was hoping there would be no need for violence today, but since you disagree..." she smirked. "Boys, if you don't mind..."

Before he could say or do anything else, two muscled men in their early twenties appeared out of nowhere and pushed him inside the house. They were wearing the same clothes: a combo of black pants and a white tank top and exhibited similar tattoos on the back of their necks. The first read "133" and the other "134". Not much of a fighter, even though he liked to pretend otherwise, Dave was easily overpowered by their efficient brutality. As he lay on the carpet, gasping for air, the woman who introduced herself as "Jane", said,

"You brought this on yourself, so don't complain. Are you ready to listen to what I have to say?"

"What do you want?" he spat fresh blood on the floor.

"All overdue mortgage payments would be nice, but let's be real here. They wouldn't have sent me if they believed they were getting their money back on such short notice. No, Mr. Sanders, I'm here to enforce clause 74a of your agreement with our institution."

"What's that?" he tried to get up, all muscles in his body in shambles as if he had been run over by a speeding train.

"Jane" produced a white sheet of paper with cursive letters written in blood-red ink and read,

"In the absence of confirmed payment of the established sum for more than three consecutive months, the institution reserves the right to take control of your body and mind in any way it sees fit for an equal period of time."

"What the hell? I don't remember signing that!" he gasped.

"No one ever reads the contracts in full, but our Legal Department is always on top of things. Your services are required, Mr. Sanders. This won't take long."

"What are you going to do?"

"You'll see," she removed her sunglasses, revealing two orbs of enchanting malice. Their ominous glow engulfed the room.

* * *

Dave was not in a good mood. In fact, he had no mood at all. His mind had been wiped clean, with no thoughts of defiance allowed to thrive inside. Dressed in black pants and a white tank top, he just had to look menacing enough and occasionally show a faulty customer what happened to those that failed to live up to their obligations. The tattoo on the back of his neck was still fresh and would go away when his debt was settled, whenever that may be. Until then, he was always on call, and "Jane" made sure he never strayed while at her service. There were still a lot of things he didn't understand, but the bank's motto was not one of them.

"One hell of a business," the commercials said. So true.

Ritual

Greta was fuming so hard it was a miracle her antics hadn't triggered the kitchen's fire alarm yet. As always, the victim was her boyfriend Jarod, who couldn't stop trying to prove his point.

"No way! I refuse to believe that. It's fucking impossible!" he exclaimed.

"For the last time, I'm not doing anything to you," she looked at him as if she were about to devour him whole. "Seriously, Jarod! This bullshit about brainwashing and mind control has got to stop. I had fun with your fantasies at first because of how out of the ordinary they were, but now they're just plain annoying! It's all you think about and it's straining our relationship to the point of rupture. I don't like being accused of things like that and if you keep on doing that, you'll soon discover I can do far worse things to you than have you sleep on the sofa. Stop, okay? Just stop."

"But..." he grumbled, confusion striking at him from every direction. He wanted to fight back again yet didn't know how.

"But nothing!" she tapped the kitchen counter with her pink acrylic nails. "I've had enough already! Either you apologize immediately for being an idiot again or you go take a breather and don't return until nightfall. I don't care where you have your lunch. I'm not cooking for you today."

"Damn it! You're impossible to talk to!" he threw his arms up in the air and headed out. "I'm leaving, but this isn't over! Not by a long shot, Greta."

"Yeah, yeah, whatever..."

He was so distraught on his way out he didn't even say a word to her sister Chloe who stood by the front door with a bewildered expression on her face. Two years younger, she was almost the spitting image of Greta save for the lighter green eyes and a tattoo of a slithering snake wrapped around her left wrist. She also seemed more rational overall though he wasn't sure of that anymore either.

"What's up with your boyfriend?" Chloe asked as soon as they were alone.

Greta hugged her by the kitchen entrance and replied, "Oh, same old... He's having another one of his identity crisis today. The poor bastard is convinced I'm mindfucking him no matter how much I tell him otherwise. It's exasperating."

"But you are mindfucking him! That's all you've been doing since you guys met."

"True, but not the way he thinks," Greta smirked, a myriad of powerful incantations at the tip of her tongue, each one more enticing than the rest.

"I don't get it, sis. If you're going to sacrifice him to your Goddess, why don't you do it already instead of confusing him every day? I'm starting to feel bad for him. It's almost torture at this point."

"I already told you why," the older sibling frowned. "It has to be on Halloween to maximize the energy release. And don't give me that shit about torture! You stand to gain from the ritual too."

Greta was correct, but that didn't stop Chloe from having occasional reservations. The prospect of eternal youth had never crossed her mind until she had discovered her sister was a witch and, even though she wasn't a part of her coven, she already knew almost as much as those who did.

"Just a few more days and this will be all over," Greta concluded. "Be patient, okay?"

"And then what?"

"I guess I'll have to find a new toy to play with. Want to go 'hunting' with me this afternoon?"

"Only if you let me pick the place."

"Deal!"

The two women hugged again and laughed, the wrinkles on their foreheads reminding them of the inexorable passage of Time. Soon, they would reverse the clock, and after that, there would be no limits. They couldn't wait.

Slavery 101

The thick pink strap-on fucked Naomi's mouth as she helplessly kneeled on the floor of her apartment. Rubber had never tasted better, and it was unlikely it ever would.

Unlike other teachers she knew, her career had always been peaceful and scandal-free, but on the last days of the first semester, she felt the tide starting to turn. The guilty party was Blair, a eighteen-year-old blonde with piercing gray eyes who had recently been transferred from a nearby school because of bad behavior. Lazy by nature, she spent most of her classes doing nothing but tease everyone else, and while she wouldn't say 'no' to the advances of an older man, anyone could see her true preferences from a mile away.

Anyone except Naomi.

Despite being a sweet woman, the Math teacher had a lousy track history when it came to relationships or connecting to other people. The nature of flirting also eluded her and so, it was no wonder she remained single way into her forties. Blair changed her perception with her intense gaze and, for the first time she remembered, the older woman began to dread what was happening to her heart and mind every time she saw her.

As the days went by, an unwanted attraction grew, and temptation drew from it to become even stronger. Aware of it, Blair started toying with her during sessions, whether that meant licking her lips when she was looking, lifting her skirt more than school policy allowed, or dangling her varnished shoes from under the table. Every seduction technique at her disposal was fair game, and all worked like a charm.

A few days before the first break of the year, the young woman made her move and showed up at her place, having exchanged her usual attire for a leather bustier and matching pants. In her right hand, she held a bag with a present she "wouldn't be able to say no to." - her exact words!

"Thank you, Blair, but this is highly unusual. You shouldn't be here," Naomi said.

"I had to. There's something really important I need to take care of before the holidays."

"What is it?"

"This," she suddenly pulled the other woman's neck towards her and kissed her, a raw display of blooming sexuality that left Naomi begging for more.

"What was that for?"

"I want you and I want you to want me too," she teased. And as she said this, it was as if her eyes grew, almost doubling to capture her undivided attention. A spiraling impression on each iris drew her in, time suspended on the verge of hypnotic trance. "Don't you want this body?"

"Yes," Naomi blurted.

"Then, you'll need to give me something in return."

"What do you want?"

"Your mind is a good place to start," she continued to pull the teacher's eyes towards their own, tethering them before she could say another word. "You are now trapped and can't look away. Your thoughts are getting foggier, your will is getting weaker. 'Resistance' is but a word whose meaning you'll soon forget. Forget for me as I offer you the kind of pleasure you never dreamed of. I want to play a game with you, but it has to be according to my rules. What I saw is law. My will is your will. Do you understand, my dribbling fool?"

"Yes, Blair, I do."

"Good. You may look at your present now."

The pink strap-on model was the young woman's favorite, and that was something all her toys - starting with her parents - agreed on. Naomi was no different. As the thrusting continued, rendering her gums completely numb, she knew she was now in a different classroom altogether and would stop at nothing to get the highest mark possible.

Wedding Vows

It was the happiest day in Samantha's life. The beautiful bride turned her head away from the window of her mother's master bedroom to look upon the hesitant man that was sneaking in silently, his face all red and sweaty, heart racing so fast its thundering echoes couldn't be ignored. With both hands on her waist as if pretending to be madder than what she really was, she asked,

"What are you doing here, Robert? You know you're not supposed to see me before the ceremony!"

"I need you," the early forties multimedia tycoon confessed, knowing in the deepest recesses of his soul that he was being entirely truthful. "I had to come right away."

"Why? Is there something wrong?"

"No. I finished my vows."

"So what? Save them for church."

"They're too important to wait," he gently bowed down before her. "Please give me the honor of reading them to you."

"Hmmm... I really shouldn't, but I'll allow it this time. I forgive you for your transgression... if they're any good," she added in a slightly darker tone that could easily be interpreted as a threat.

"Thank you. May I begin?"

"Yes. Get on with it before my sisters return."

Removing a piece of perfumed paper from the outer pocket of his classic black tux, he began to read with surprising conviction,

"I choose you, my beloved, to be my wife. To live with you and for you; to stand by your side and sleep in your arms; to be joy to your heart and food to your soul; to bring out the best in you always just like you do in me. To wed the person your heart truly desires is unparalleled bliss. I vow that henceforth, my heart will be your shelter. As I have given you my hand to hold, I give you my life to keep forever."

She smiled openly and his knees buckled forward,

"Not bad. They could be better, but I think they're perfect enough to convince everyone attending that this is a standard marriage. Of course, we both know the truth, don't we?"

A speck of light bounced off her tiara to land on his eyes, overflowing with adoration, a gaze that responded to her jewelry the same way a computer program responds to the instructions given by its user. He had been well trained. Without another word, he dropped to kiss her pearly feet.

"What if someone sees you?" she smirked.

"I don't care. You're my mistress, my goddess. I want to worship you all day long."

"You'll have the rest of your life for that, my brainwashed thrall," she lowered her right hand to cup his chin. "Right now, I need you to get back to your room and keep the schedule going as planned."

"Please, Mistress... just one kiss..."

"I already said no, pet. Leave me be or I'll have to punish you."

"And if I do this?" he buried his head under her pristine dress until his lips tasted her sweet stockinged pussy.

"You're really pushing your luck. I may have to fry your brains again for such audacity," she giggled.

"Yes, please!" his teeth gnawed at the white stocking's seams.

Samantha leaned against the window and moaned as he did what he knew best. His tongue was too good to go to waste. They would be running a little late, after all.

You Want to Be a Good Girl

You want to be a good girl.

You need to be a good girl.

You will be a good girl for me.

Look at the spiral before your eyes.

Look deep into the center of the spiral.

It's red like the dress I would like you to imagine right now.

It's a short, slutty dress, hugging every curve of your beautiful body.

A dress that will make everyone's heads turn and make them lust for you with every step you take.

It's the dress I want all good girls of mine to use in order to please me.

You want to be a good girl.

You need to be a good girl.

You will be a good girl for me.

See this dress I just described right in the center of the spiral.

The more you look at it the clearer it becomes while everything else fades away.

When you stare at the spiral and your imagination works with me, you needn't think about anything else.

Whatever was on the edge of your thoughts before you started listening to me is no more.

There's only the red spiral.

There's only the dress waiting in its center.

There's only the need to touch it and feel the soft fabric against your naked skin.

Do it now.

Stretch out your hands and grab it.

Pull the dress into the real world and hold like it's the most precious thing in the world because it is.

I've chosen it for you so you can be my good girl.

You want to be a good girl.

You need to be a good girl.

You will be a good girl for me.

Good girls stand on their toes to try out the dress.

It's okay if you need to look away from the spiral to do this for it will still be spinning in your mind.

The spiral never stops, and neither does the urge to give in to my desires.

Smell the dress and let it intoxicate your senses.

Yes, take a deep breath and soak it all in.

It smells of power, control, and unbridled sex.

The scent is so intense it's borderline irresistible.

The moment you put on this dress, all the sexual energy within it will be channeled into you.

You will become submerged in it, wanting nothing more than to surrender and obey.

No thoughts.

No inhibitions.

No resistance.

A puppet on the spiraling dance-floor created for my amusement.

You will become a good girl.

Everyone will want you.

Everyone will fight for a chance to be with you.

Everyone will yearn to take you... and you'll let them.

That's what good girls do.

You want to be a good girl.

You need to be a good girl.

You will be a good girl for me.

Put it on now.

Doll yourself up to achieve perfection.

The world is waiting for its new horny fucktoy, and it's waited long enough.

Put it on and let me see how you look.

Perfect.

You never looked better, for now you're complete.

Good boys make the best girls when they're entranced, and you're no exception.

This is what you want to be. You accept it now.

You want to be a good girl.

You need to be a good girl.

You will be a good girl for me for the rest of your life.

About the author

S.B., Simple Being, middle name Creative. Writer and artist with a penchant for themes of Femdom Hypnosis and Mind Control. His thoughts are his own except when they're not.

Besides indulging himself in kinky delights, he loves his furry family of two (dogs), sci-fi and horror stories, and puns galore. He's also been writing a piece of erotic micro-fiction every single day since January 1st, 2016 and has no intention of stopping anytime soon.

Find out more and keep up with his latest extravaganzas by visiting and supporting his personal website, Spell... B-O-U-N-D.

www.ingramcontent.com/pod-product-compliance
Lightning Source LLC
Chambersburg PA
CBHW071456150726
48000CB00006B/2582